archyology

# archyology

the long lost tales of archy and mehitabel

## don marquis

edited and with a preface by jeff adams

with drawings by ed frascino

university press of new england

hanover and london

for yvette and harry adams

published by university press of new england

one court street, lebanon, nh 03766

www.upne.com

this compilation copyright © 1996 by jeff adams

drawings copyright © 1996 by ed frascino

first university press of new england paperback edition 2009

printed in the united states of america   5  4  3  2  1

isbn for paperback edition: 978–1–58465–806–1

cip data appear at the end of the book

designed by mike burton

university press of new england is a member of the green press
initiative. the paper used in this book meets their
minimum requirement for recycled paper.

# contents

# preface

For much of his working life, Don Marquis, considered by some to have been the successor to Mark Twain as America's foremost literary wit, was a daily newspaper columnist for the *New York Sun* and later the *Herald Tribune*. Marquis was by nature a poet whose feelings for language and life — and his imaginative, humorous expressions of those feelings — contributed largely to his popularity.

Faced with the constant need for new material to fill his column, Marquis invented a number of fictional characters through which his opinions on the issues of the day could be expressed.

His two most enduring characters are Archy the Cockroach and Mehitabel the Alley Cat, who made their first appearance in March 1916 and continued to surface in a wide variety of publications into the 1930s.

Archy claimed to be a long departed poet whose soul had transmigrated into the body of a lowly cockroach. Each night his "boss" (Marquis) left a sheet of paper in his typewriter so that Archy, leaping headfirst from carriage to key, could bang out his observations one painful lowercase letter at a time. Archy's soulmate was Mehitabel the Alley Cat, a free-spirited feline who claimed to have once been Cleopatra. Archy dutifully chronicled her adventures, along with his own and those of many other colorful characters.

Don Marquis died over a half century ago. At that time, many of his manuscripts and scrapbooks were simply gathered together, locked in a steamer trunk, and stored in a

Brooklyn warehouse. Among those papers were literally hundreds of Archy and Mehitabel stories. Several years ago, the warehouse was cleared. Usable items, like the trunk, were saved. Suddenly, after so much time, the Marquis archive again saw the light of day. I examined the archive and made this lucky discovery: a great number of these "lost" tales of Archy and Mehitabel had never before been published in a collection. You are now holding that collection.

The verses in this book are classic Archy and Mehitabel. They will make you smile, but be warned—they will also make you think.

JEFF ADAMS

archyology

# and so

in reply to all
the clamor and queries
as to where i
have been and what i
have been doing i will
make but two
comments the
first one is can a
public character have no
privacy at all and the
second is why should not
even a cockroach take a rest

archy

# what next

transmigration
of souls
is a great game
if you do not weaken
but every
now and then
i get worried
about my future
i used to be
a vers libre poet
before my ego went into
the body of a cockroach
and some times i turn
pale with the
thought that i may
be going further down
yet before i start
to climb back
i might even
be a hat check boy
in a hotel

archy

# mehitabel s motto

i had a serious talk
with our friend mehitabel recently
and i am very much afraid boss
that she will never reform
domesticity never
appealed to me archy
she told me
i know a lot of tame tabbies
and what do they get
out of life
nothing my dear
but respectability
and a sense of superiority
life for them is just
one damned kitten after another
and they have no medium
for self expression
but me exclamation point
i am free as the air
i live for art
it is better to be found frozen
in an alley and go down the bay
in a garbage scow
than to be afraid
to kick your heels up on the floor
for fear of what the tabby
next door will think
do not pity my way of life
i live as the gods ordained i should
i am never so happy

as when i am broke
and lately i have been happy all the time
expression expression
my life is all expression

does the warm fireside
and a silken rug
and cream and oysters
at regular hours never appeal
to you mehitabel i ask her
i have had all those things archy
she said and i left them
for the lure of adventure
romance or nothing is my motto
today i am up tomorrow i am down

but i am always gay
and always the lady
do you never have any
qualms of conscience
with regard to your unconventionalities
i asked her
what i am i am exclamation point
she said
and if there were more
like me in the world
heaven forbid i said interrupting her
the secret of life
as i have found it she said
is always to shoot the whole roll
never go in for half measures

in anything
this principle has no doubt led
to your success in life i said
with veiled irony
yes she said quite complacently
as she struggled with
an ancient fish bone
i owe all that i am to these
principles
boss what are you going to do
with these spirits
who are miserable
and do not know it
who are iniquitous and proud of it
who are pitiable
and boast of their condition
who are defeated
and believe themselves victorious
who are corrupt
and contented
who are undeserving
and talk of their principles
who are unconscious that they should repent
who are disreputable
and gay
it is a problem i pass along
to the sociologists

        archy

that cockroach glide

boss you oughta been
here last night we
had a ball on
top of your desk in honor
of your getting it cleaned
for 1917 three
cockroaches a katydid

two spiders and a
peruvian flea that came
in with the decayed
gentleman who tried to sell
you his autobiography in
poetical form the
other day and compromised by
borrowing a dime finally
a thousand legs came along
and made a hit by
dancing a dozen different
dances all at once each
pair of legs keeping step to a
different tune what we
need here worst of
all is two or three crickets
for an orchestra i
am inventing a new
step called that cockroach
glide

                    archy

# archy insists

well boss you have
a nerve to turn down
my modest
request for a little
trip to paris
have you reflected
how much i
could tell about you
i do not wish
to use strong arm
methods or
anything that could
be construed as
blackmail but i
will tell the
world who does all your
thinking for you
and a good part
of your writing
unless you make
immediate arrangements
to take me on a
little trip
i don t care what
it costs you
i need a change of
scene and a change
of air i need
some new interests
my health is suffering

from continual
over work for years
this is my
last word to you
and a verb
to any sap should
be sufficient
remember i will tell
all

                    archy

All right, then, little cockroach, we will take you to Paris
some time or other! It is not that you have intimidated us,
we have nothing to conceal that you might reveal; but there
is, after all, a certain justice in your demands. We <u>have</u>
worked you pretty hard for a number of years, and it is only
right that you should have something in the way of compen-
sation.

# wish i were keats

oh list
to the call of
the springtime
oh hark to
suggestions of may
awake for its
birds on the
wing time give
ear for the meadows
are gay which
also applies to the tearooms
the boulevards
avenues

streets
the dear rooms and cheap
rooms and free rooms for
spring is a season
of sweets oh god
but i wish i were keats
oh god but i
wish i were
keats
oh spring s a
success as a season though
summer and winter
must come bum bum and
that is the principal
reason i m glad that i
wasn t born dumb bum bum
i m glad that
i wasn t born
dumb
you have my permission
to slap that into your so
called column
just so long as you don t
crowd it
into nonpareil or some
such illegible
infinitesimal
openly decimal type
you snipe
i can t keep from rhyming
and metering and
everything
better have it set in
that eighteen point bold
they use for headlines

archy

# plaint of spring

why do not any of
you poets tell the truth
about spring all i ever hear
of is violets and
jonquils and crocuses and
swallows and so forth
not a word of sooty
snow and melancholy
suburbs and downtown
alleys sweating mud
and influenza germs taking a
new lease of life
and winter underwear
beginning to itch along
the human shin

and snakes beginning to crawl
out from under
strawstacks in the country
and livers turning
grouchy and granddad feeling
so young in the noonday
sun that he overdoes himself
and then has to go to
bed with the lumbago
and pneumonia suddenly
rushing back after
everybody has thought it was
gone for good and
kicking people unexpectedly
in the unprotected lungs
and peach trees
starting to bud and getting
frozen to death and
business men making
love to stenographers they
do not really
give a damn about and
getting in bad and
messy back yards
with sore eyed cats
in them cursing the march
moon at midnight
and no bock beer
anywhere any more
and everything why do
not the poets
try to tell the truth
yours till prohibition
prohibits

                    archy

# all the french

"Archy," we said to that intelligent little insect yesterday, "this trip to Paris that you have forced us into is assuming grand proportions now that Mehitabel the Cat has also served an ultimatum on us.

"What sort of spectacle will we present, descending upon Paris with this parade at our heels — the trained Cockroach and Mehitabel the Cat? And how the deuce are we going to get along over there, anyhow? We don't know a word of French?"

Archy ambled over to the typewriter and bumped out the following reply:

> you don t need
> to know but a
> few words of
> french i have
> been to paris
> before and all the
> french an american
> needs to know
> there is
> combyang
> which means
> how much and
> when you say that
> he says how
> much it is
> and then you say

15

tray chair
which means it is
too much
and then he says
how much it is
again and then
you say
beaucoo tray chair
which means
it is too dam much
and then he
says how much it
is again
and then you
pay what he says
that is all
the french you need
to know

Encouraged by this, we began to consider the idea more
seriously.

# paris or bust

We received the following communication from Archy:

> dear boss what
> is the matter with you
> are you trying
> to squirm out of
> that little jaunt to
> paris that you
> promised me
> get busy at once and
> make the arrangements
> or i will
> tell all
>
> archy

Every honorable man is forced to yield to blackmail once or twice in his life, just for the sake of keeping peace in the community.

So we asked Archy to develop his ideas a little more. He replied:

> i want to go as
> soon as possible
> and i want to go
> on the cunard line
> and i want to go
> on one of their ships

and i want to go as
soon as possible

Accordingly, we went downtown to the offices of the Cunard Line. They advised the Tyrrhenia.

"How many in your party?" asked the gentlemanly clerk.

"Well," we said, "besides us there's Mehitabel and Archy."

"Archy?" The clerk looked up from the plan of the ship with a speculative eye. "You don't mean Archy the Cockroach?"

"None other," we replied proudly. The clerk shook his head sadly. "I'm afraid it is impossible," he said. "The Cunard Line has never yet carried a cockroach, and it never can. A cockroach on the Cunard Line is unthinkable."

"But Archy isn't an ordinary cockroach," we pleaded.

"There has never been a cockroach on a Cunard ship," repeated the clerk with more determination than ever, "and there never will be one."

All we could do was to go back and report the situation to Archy. He hopped over to the typewriter and wrote:

i told you before
i don t care what
the expenses are
buy a ship if necessary
go i will and go i
must

archy

Finally we hit on a compromise. We telephoned the clerk

in the Cunard offices that we wouldn't go unless we went by
his line, and asked if it wouldn't be possible to attach a small
vessel as a trailer to the Tyrrhenia for Archy.

So the matter has been arranged on that basis. The trailer
will also accommodate Mehitabel the Cat, for she wishes to
be with Archy.

Archy has been provided with a special typewriter and his
own vessel has been equipped with wireless apparatus so
that, if the spirit moves him, he may send back bulletins of
his progress. We are sailing this afternoon.

# over the limit

special dispatch
to home
by radio
from the trailer
attached to
cunard liner
tyrrhenia
we passed the
three mile
limit some

time ago and
the old shoak
was already
she shick

archy

# archy repels an attack of whales

by radio from
the trailer attached
to the cunard liner
tyrrhenia north
atlantic ocean august
thirteenth nineteen
hundred twenty three
i passed a night of
sleeplessness and perturbation
last night
this vessel in which
mehitabel the cat
and i are
crossing the ocean
was surrounded by whales
shortly after midnight
the head whale came
and peered over the
gunwale of our
little vessel with a
fiery eye
and following him
were countless other
whales waiting on his
command
to starboard to port
and in our wake
were hordes

of whales
whales whales whales
as far as the eye could
reach and all of
them wore an angry air
in the starlight
to say that i
felt helpless is to
put it mildly
you may laugh at my
fears but you have
never been a cockroach in
a small boat
attacked in the middle
of a vast ocean by
thousands of whales
at midnight
sir i said to the head
whale is there no way
that two gentlemanly
disposed insects can settle
this matter by honorable
compromise he gave a
bellow of rage and
opened his mouth half the way
from labrador to the
panama canal i thought
that all was lost i said
hastily pardon me i did
not mean to call you an insect
it was only a slip of the
tongue as if mollified he
closed his mouth
sir i said i will be
coming back this way in two
or three months and if
there is anything i

can bring you please let
me know he answered never a
word but he and his tens of
thousands of followers came
steadily on relentlessly on
sir i said consider
before you act rashly
we are both god s creatures
you and i i am small and
you are large but the same
life force animates us both
we have no doubt to a
considerable degree
the same affections
and sympathies the same loves
and troubles
my dear sir i do not wish

to be impertinent
but do you have a mother
he gave a great sob and sank
beneath the waves all the

other whales sobbed and sank
beneath the waves
a million whales sobbing
in the moonlight
is an impressive sight
when they arose from the
water again
their eyes i saw were wet
i wish the boss would put a
sentimental effect of that kind
in his next play
sir i continued to the whale
i have a mother too
or rather i said
permitting my voice to break
i once had a mother
they sobbed again it made me
feel like a poet
reading his poem
to a rotary club
your mother i continued may be
waiting at home for you
waiting for you to return
as pure and bright eyed and
innocent as when she sent you
forth can you return to her
stained with the crime of my
murder and look her in the eye
they sobbed once more
and sank
thus i talked with them
all through the night
appealing to their better
natures and when the first
red streaks of dawn
showed over the horizon
they disappeared

it was mentality working upon
matter that saved us
but mehitabel the cat says
it was sentimentality
working on blubber
but i shall never say
another word
against a whale
my nerves
and the sea are
very sick of
each other i hope i do
not meet any icebergs how
would one talk an iceberg out
of it

              archy

# captain s progress

by wireless to home
north atlantic ocean
august fifteenth
i am afraid our captain
is an awful four flush
i crawled up the cable
from my trailer
to the big ship last night
and heard him
bragging to a new found friend
that he was a great aviator

why said the captain
i once crossed the
english channel
upside down
that is nothing said
the other man i once
crossed the atlantic ocean
practically inside out
the captain became angry
and flung his card down
let me see said the other
man putting on his eye glasses
and looking at the card
what are you selling
sir said the captain
if i had you on my
dueling barge
instead of this ship you
would sing another tune
the man then sung
another tune in a
mocking manner the
song was something about
bananas but i did
not catch the purport
but when i left the
captain had pardoned him
and was telling him about
an opera he had written
and calling him old man

archy

# mehitabel at sea

on board the
trailer following
the tyrrhenia
by wireless to
home august
sixteen
a man
just now looked over
the rail of the big
ship ahead he seemed to
be very sad about something
why are you so sad
i asked him
i am sad
he replied because
one cannot eat
ones cake
and keep it too
we passed
a buoy a while ago
that had broken
away from its
moorings what is
that said an
old maid
that is one of
the buoys said
mehitabel it is on
the loose i suppose
some mermaid

will grab that buoy
you horrid thing
said the old prude
well said mehitabel

buoys will be buoys
and you
should not be
so inimical to
mermaids they
haven t any legs

archy

# archy reaches paris

paris france
august seventeenth
nineteen hundred and
twenty three
we arrived in paris
just now and the
procession will pass
through the principal streets
up to the
time of putting this
on the wire
we have not been
met by the president
of france
nor in fact anything
at all in the way
of a reception
committee i cannot
understand it
i wish to be quiet and
inconspicuous but i
had not thought i would
be entirely ignored
as we came out
of the railroad station
we met two
johndarms and asked them
if there was a
knights of pythias
convention going on

in town but fortunately
we were not understood
do not expect too much
from me for a few days

archy

# what can a lady do

paris france
august twenty third
by archygram to
home
mehitabel the cat
has disappeared i
do not wish to be
an alarmist
but it seems possible
to me that she may have
been abducted again
she had a series of
terrible experiences in
new york some years ago
she was abducted and
abducted and abducted
again and again and again
but the police
refused to
take it seriously
she said to me
archy fate is
a terrible thing
no one can dodge his or
her fate
it seems to be my
fate to be abducted
continually
what can a lady do
i am helpless in the

grip of circumstances
if it must happen it
must
the only thing a lady
can do

archy
is to pick out her
abductor
and i am very much
afraid that mehitabel
has assisted in her own
abduction
this is practically
archy week in paris

archy

# aunt prudence hecklebury

aunt prudence hecklebury
lies on her bed
moaning and groaning
wishing she were dead
aunt prudence hecklebury
tosses on her couch
and all that she says
is ouch ouch ouch
aunt prudence hecklebury
rouses and screams
when the sights she has seen
move through her dreams
first aunt prudence
went to the louvre
then wrote the government
that they really should remove
some of those statues
right out of france
or else give them skirts
or else give them pants
skirts on the venus
pants on apollo
a great moral uplift
surely would follow
maybe the government
never got the note
for the louvre is just the same
as before she wrote
aunt prudence hecklebury
rode around town

with her whole being twisted
into a frown
aunt prudence hecklebury
moans and twitches
wakes now and then
and cries out breeches
o give them breeches
please give them breeches
aunt prudence hecklebury

on her bed of pain
screams now and then
and clutches her brain
for aunt prudence went
to the follies bergere
mother hubbard s cupboard
wasn t half as bare
some wear smiles
and some wear paint
but otherwise their clothes
just simply aint
dear aunt prudence
why did you do it
prudence prudence prudence
i knew that you d rue it
in a lucid moment
she said after this
i hardly know whether
to call myself miss
she saw what she saw
and she heard what she heard
and limbs aint the word for it
limbs aint the word
aunt prudence hecklebury
in her darkened room
murmurs there is rest
only in the tomb
she saw what she saw
and she heard what she heard
and nude aint the word for it
nude aint the word
aunt prudence hecklebury
fevered on her couch
her whole being s turned
into an ouch

                    archy

# archy figures out aunt prudence

Aunt Prudence Hecklebury does not approve of Archy, and
Archy has been wondering why. Yesterday, however, he had
a flash of insight and wrote:

> i know why
> aunt prudence hecklebury
> does not like me
> period
> it came to me
> just now
> exclamation point
> it is because
> i have six
> legs
> exclamation point
> please ask her if
> this is not so
> interrogation point
> if she disapproves
> of me for that
> reason what
> are her views
> with regard to
> the octopus
> question mark
> and i shudder to
> think of what
> she must think
> when she sees

a centipede
period

archy

# idle thought

paris september
fifth nineteen
twenty three
what i like
about this place
is that it is
such a nice
place to loaf in
and loafing
is the best thing
in life
nature shows
us that
a caterpillar
 just eats and
  loafs and sleeps
  and after a while
  without any effort
  it turns into
  a butterfly

with nothing to do
but flit around
and be beautiful
but consider
the industrious
tumble bug
the tumble bug
toils and plants
and sweats
and worries
pushing its burden
up hill forever
like sisyphus
and pretty soon
some one
comes along
and thinks how
vulgar and ugly
the thing is
and steps on it
and squashes it
idleness
and beauty
are their own
rewards
mehitabel the cat
is still missing

                    archy

# diplomacy

paris september
twenty third i was
talking today with a wise
old cockroach
who is known as
gaston le cafard
who claims he has helped
formulate the
foreign policies of france
for many years
i have seen presidents
and premiers come and go
archy he said many oh very
many of them i have
lived on and about
the quai dorsay
for decades
the most disturbing thing
in all my experience
has been the advent of
your brutal american
diplomacy in europe
you go about the most
serious affairs with the most
distressing directness
you have no conception of
that subtlety that finish
which matters of the most
importance demand
i can see what gaston le cafard

means for example it
was only the other day
when the belgian premier
wished to discuss with
monsieur poincare
some phases of the ruhr situation
but did he come to paris
to consult with
monsieur poincare
he did not he shrouded
the whole matter in the most
agreeable and romantic mystery
he came to paris
to attend the wedding of the fifth
cousin of his uncle s
great aunt s nephew s daughter
and quite by accident
quite by the happiest
and most unforeseen coincidence
he ran across monsieur poincare
in paris and they were guests
at the same luncheon party
and what more natural than
that they should both speak
of the subject which occupies their
thoughts and what they spoke
remains to this day
a profound secret
except to the newspaper correspondents
who told it to the reading
publics of all the nations in
europe the two americas
asia africa and australia
but the traditions of european
diplomacy remain unbroken
some day prime minister baldwin
will find in his heart a

great yearning to sit on the
top of an alp in switzerland
and fish for yodelers
with swiss cheese sandwiches
and he will suddenly discover
a strange gentleman is sitting
on the other side
of a boulder feeding crumbs
from a bun to the eagles
and behold it will be
monsieur poincare
and what more natural
than that these two
distinguished gentlemen so
fortunately met upon their
pleasant holidays should fall into
talk concerning mussolini

reparations and what not
and how are they to blame
if their secretaries are on hand
with megaphones
to shout their conclusions

to the reporters waiting in
the vale below again the
traditions of european diplomacy
will have been preserved
subtlety that is the word
subtlety and secrecy and dignity
and indirection
i agree entirely with gaston le cafard
that we americans are crude
in our methods
i asked him what he thought
of the league of nations
america has killed it by
staying out of it thank god
he said if she had come into
it it would have been
harder to kill
the great thing now
that it is safely dead is to
pretend that it is still
alive diplomatic occasions
will undoubtedly arise when
the corpse can be used to advantage
the great misfortune would be a candid
and decent burial
now that it is dead it comes
well within the scope
of matters that can be safely
handled by the european
diplomatists the situation
was always full of danger so long
as it was alive and we
were forced to pretend that we
wished to keep it alive
i said but it really died
when it refused
to handle mussolini

hush he said that talk
shows how crude an american you are
we know that it is dead
but we must not say that it is dead
for some day we shall need
to galvanize the corpse
temporarily for a week or two
but also there will be times
when without saying it is dead
we will proceed upon the tacit
assumption that it is dead
and at those times the corollary
assumption will be
that america killed it
the safest plan is to say nothing
at all about it right now
and to say it secretly and publicly
at great length i hope you
understand me i do not
i said ah said gaston le cafard
you are becoming subtle yourself

archy

# the insects of europe

paris october
eleventh at home i
used to see a lot of eloquent
appeals in the papers
from gentlemen and ladies
with noble and philanthropic
hearts the burden
of which was that it was up
to america quotation marks
to save europe end quotes
i have talked
with a number of insects
here in paris
from all over europe
and they all admit
they would like
to have their countries
saved by america but the
trouble seems to be
that each one wants his country
saved at the expense
of somebody else
apostrophe s country
gaston le cafard
my friend from the quai
d apostrophe orsay
points out to me however
that france does not want anybody
to save her she has
buckled down and worked

like hades for several years
now and has raised everything her
people want to eat
and has saved herself
our army says gaston
is for the purpose of
keeping ourselves saved
gaston assures me privately

that in his opinion france
will likely save the slice of germany
she now occupies until
germany saves herself
by saving enough money
to do something in the way
of reparations
an italian cockroach informed
me that in his estimation

it would be very nice
if america saved europe
but in the meantime
he thought it likely that
italy would save all she could
get away from greece
in the way of lire
and that it was still an open
question whether greece
or italy would save corfu
you see the spirit that prevails
on this continent
they all want to save each other
as they can
the jugo slavs
a centipede from that
region tells me
would like to save an outlet
from the adriatic sea
but they fear that
mussolini intends sooner or later
to save the adriatic
in the name of italy
there is always the chance
for a good deal of salvage
in those regions
it is my own opinion
that the european nations
are so chronically eager
to save one another
that it is almost an impertinence
on the part of america
to butt into the situation
and do any saving
the english i am informed
are very low
in their minds as to the

possibility of saving
british trade industry and
so forth but it will probably
be discovered later
that they have saved
a good deal in one way
or the other
a water bug from london
is my authority
for the statement that
the british usually emerge
from a period
of terrible dejection
with something valuable
in their hands
and are never afterwards able
to explain just how it got there
they were thinking
what an awful hole
the empire was in
and when they woke up
they discovered that while
they were brooding in despair
somehow or other
they had annexed
some more territory
or acquired some valuable
concessions
or negotiated
some advantageous treaties
or something
and always without
any deliberate intention
on their part
they function instinctively

archy

# archy explains the romanoffs

paris france jan seven nine
teen nineteen well boss
today i feel somewhat
solemn yesterday i
stood at the tomb of
napoleon and beside me stood
the man who would be
nicholas of russia and
czar of all the romanoffs
if he had his rights and
we exchanged thoughts
on kings past present and future
i am king in abeyance
said the czar i am a
has been but i will come again
all i want is enough
money to get my trunks from
siberia and my other clothes to
appear before the peace
conference and have my claims
recognized alas to lose a great
empire through lack of a
few paltry yards of cloth and a clean
collar and he wept for a
moment dash bracket first i
must tell you how the czar and i
are able to talk with one
another i have six legs as you
may have noticed each leg stands
for four letters of the

alphabet for instance the left
upper leg is a b c and d
when i point up with it that is
a when i point down with it
it is b when i point to the right
that is c when i point to
the left that is d the
left centre leg stands for
e f g and h the left lower
leg stands for i j k l and
so on with the right upper right
centre and right lower legs
there are twenty six letters in the
alphabet and i can only represent
twenty four of them so i
get along without sometimes
w and y bracket dash
the czar wept for a moment and
then he said archy the
romanoffs were kings when the
bonapartes were running a
boarding house in corsica but
behold the two of us
napoleon and nicholas both down
and out archy misfortune is
the great leveler in the
old days my great grandfather
used to let his servants
board with the bonapartes
while he stayed in a swell
hotel when he visited corsica for the
fishing season but now
napoleon and i are down and
out together and of
equal rank alas for royalty no
matter how a family gets
it it is hard to keep archy as

i stand here and think
of the troubles of royalty i
am almost tempted never to be a
king again i sometimes
think it would be better to
get a job somewhere and work
at it if it were not
for my unhappy people i would
make no effort to come
back napoleon was an
usurper and i was a
legitimate monarch but as i
look upon his urn archy i
can not but pity him archy
there is one thing i want to speak
to you about while i think
of it if you are going to
continue to travel with
me please do not stick your
head out of my pocket to
listen when i speak to new
acquaintances that marine who
was going to lend me five
francs the other day saw you
peeping out of my pocket and it
gave him the idea
that perhaps i had fleas or
something also and he
hurried away you see my
clothing is in disrepair and
people get ideas if they see you i
missed getting that five franc piece
and i had intended to
buy stamps with it and write
a special delivery letter to siberia
for my other clothes in
which to appear before the

peace conference to think that
the indiscretions of a
cockroach might lose a man
an empire but it was the
same way with napoleon
here my grandfather told me
that napoleon had the
itch and that all through the
battle of waterloo when
he should have been looking at
maps and things and

giving orders he was scratching
himself if he could have
kept his mind on the battle he
would have won it as usual to
think of it one great empire lost
on account of a cockroach and
another because of a
little skin eruption luck archy luck
rules the world and
most of mine had been bad
lately czar i said i do not
believe in luck if you
had worked harder on the job
and if napoleon here had not
got the swell head you both
might have kept your empires it
was your mistakes that
ditched you yes napoleon did make
mistakes said the czar one
of them was the time he invaded
russia it was a breach of
faith grandfather romanoff used to
say but he forgave him and as i
look upon his urn here
and think how luck has laid
him low i forgive him too us
romanoffs always were kind hearted
that way often i have
heard grandfather romanoff tell
how he repelled the
invasion at the head of his
troops he and napoleon met at
the entrance of the kremlin
and both drew their swords and
rushed at each other
but bonaparte was not as good
a fencer as my

grandfather romanoff he came of
a middle class family and had few
advantages in his youth the
first lick he struck went
wild and you can see the
nick his sword made in the
front door of the kremlin to
this day grandfather romanoff
disarmed him and might
have killed him but the
romanoffs were always the soul of
chivalry he handed napoleon s
sword back to him and said i
will give you another chance just then
the snow began to fall and
fell in a blinding storm they
fought for two hours in a snow
so dense they could not see
each other s faces but only the
sword blades and the sparks from
their swords melted the snow that
touched them and they fought in
fog and steam my
grandfather romanoff wounded
him nine times and beat him
back and he left russia at once
but moscow had been ignited
by the sparks and the greater part
of it burned

                    archy

# the famous fish of the seine

paris october sixth
i saw in a french
paper the other day that
the humane society of
santa barbara california
had protested
against the introduction of
mexican jumping
beans into california
it seems they set
them in the hot sun and
after a while they begin
to jump
the thing that makes
them jump is the fact
that they are full of insects
and the insects
suffer with the heat
and become agitated
the humane society is very
properly exercised
over this brutality to the poor
little insects
i wish they had the proper
feeling about
insects in this country
but they are not nearly so humane
here the cockroaches
i have met tell me
that they get practically

no protection from the law
they must trust
for immunity from attack
to make personal friends
of the families in which they live
and this is not
in all cases possible
sometimes after feeding
and flattering
a cockroach for weeks
a french family

will decide to go fishing
and take him over to
the seine and use him for bait
they are forever
trying to find some new sort
of bait with which to catch
the one fish which
legend says lives in the seine
you see hundreds
fishing for this fish
every day
the last time a fish was
caught there was during the
reign of louis quinze
and then they illuminated
the louvre and pulled
a te deum in notre dame
napoleon built
the arc de triomphe
in the expectation
that the remaining fish
would be caught
and the plans for a great
public festival were already made
it was planned that
the fish was to be
borne through the arch
at the head of the army
but napoleon s regime ended
with the fish of the seine
still uncaptured
and he used to sit on
his lonely rock by the sad
sea shore at saint helena
and brood over it
and the commune ended
the reign of napoleon third

the tuileries because he had
not made good on his promise
to capture the fish
who is said to live in the seine
there are fishermen
who have no other vocation
they are pledged
by their parents early in
life to fish in the seine
as if they were joining some
esoteric order and they fish
contentedly from the age of four
to the age of one hundred and four
now and then one of
them hooks into the clothing
of some person
who has loved not wisely but
too well and brings his or her
body to the surface
but this is the nearest they ever
come to catching a fish
but they are never discouraged
the arch type of quiet and placid
optimism is the fisherman
of the seine hope is theirs that
renews itself
from itself
eternally nobody can become
president of the republic
unless he stands bareheaded in
the place de la concorde
and swears with his hand
upon the place where
the guillotine
used to stand
that he believes there is a fish

in the seine
this great faith affects
even foreigners
i find myself believing
in the possibility
of there really being a fish
in the seine since i last
wrote you mehitabel the cat
has made up with
francy again
and they have moved
from the catacombs to montmartre

                              archy

# all for science

boss my interest in science
is keen but my
sympathy with scientists is
declining very rapidly the
more i see of them the less i
want them to see
me i heard a couple of
entomologists talking the
other day you want to be sure
and get over to the brooklyn
museum on thursday evening he said
there is going to be a
lecture on a new
kind of bug killer good
said the second one i will
surely be there if there is
anything that is needed for
the cause right now
it is a new bug killer i
looked at him and he
seemed a kind hearted man too
just thoughtless likely
i thought what is sport to
you old fellow is
death to us insects morality
is all in the point
of view if the cockroaches
should start killing the
humans just to study them there
would a howl go up from

danville illinois to
beersheba palestine many would
think twice about stepping
on a pacifist who would
send any number of potato bugs
to their funeral pyre without
remorse justice as maurice
maeterlinck points out is not
inherent in the universe and what
man has put there he
uses when he uses it at all
strictly for his own
purposes the world is so sad that
the only way to live
with it is to laugh at it

                              archy

# archy the cockroach turns detective

listen to me
you know that fellow that was
in to see you last week and said
he would go to jail if he did
not get 30 dollars by 3 p m to make

up to his bank the rest of a check he had
cashed because the check was too
big for his balance and his
wife was sick in the hospital
well after you lent him
that 1 dollar i crawled
into his overcoat that was on
a chair hunting candy because he
said he had promised to bring some home
to his baby girl who
cries for her sick
mother all the time and had
spent his last cent for some well
there was no candy in his overcoat
pockets and i went to sleep
there while listening to you and him
bull each other it bored me and
when i woke i was in a gin
palace listen now your friend
was waited for there the fellow
who was waiting says to him did
that simp fall for you
one lonely little buck
says your friend god hates
a tightwad says your friend s friend
amen says your friend what will
it be drink up your friend s friend drank
up and told a hard luck tale he
says i tried to touch a boob
and he offered me a
job it s getting dangerous
well i heard enough talk to
see there was no truth in
that sick wife story i crawled
to the street listen i
was up near columbus circle it
took me 6 days to get back i

get into the subway and managed to
get into an express at grand central
that was where i made my mistake i
couldn t get off again at the bridge the
doors would close every time before i
could get off i had to watch
everybody s step at once
a guard tried to strafe me for
4 days i kept being carried past
brooklyn bridge up and down up
and down and at last walked from
the brooklyn end of the line and
so home and to bed

archy

# archy crawls among the h s

i don t know
what you were
looking up on that
page of the dictionary
you left it open at

but i have gleaned
some interesting
information from it
and i want to
thank you you dropped
a piece of cracker

on the page and
i crawled up to get
it for my supper
tonight
on the way i
had to walk across
a lot of words
among them i stepped
on heretic which
is spending quite a
lot of time on front
pages these days
the dictionary says
heretic a holder of
an unorthodox opinion
do you know anybody
who isn t a heretic
i don t

archy

# georgie the college centipede

i am georgie
the biggest and most intelligent
centipede on the
college campus
i am a roving
soul
a nomad so
to speak my particular
hobby is to crawl
down the wall
after the girl
whose room i
happen to be in
has gone to bed
to study
she ought not
to do that
anyway i say
to myself it s
bad for her eyes
so out of compassion
for her i balance
myself above her
head and start
down the wall
i seldom get far
before she shrieks
oh exclamation point
help help help
and jumps out of

68

bed most immodestly
this is the only thanks i
ever get for my
thoughtfulness
but what can you
expect from the
products of this
higher education
at vassar college
they argue on free
love or marriage
labor or capital
democracy or autocracy
christianity or paganism
to be or not to be
but they always
see both sides of
every question
perfectly
and it makes them
feel far away
and impersonal
and sort of
detached from everything
except abstract truths
they haven t any
passions or even
any feelings except
stark terror
at the sight of
my pal
christabel the rat
i verily believe she
has more power and
prestige with the college
girls than the president
himself

though of course i would
never let him know
i thought so
it s too great a
blow underlined
to a man apostrophe s
pride
to see a woman
influence other women
more than he can
himself how does she
do it i ask
question mark
that has been and still is
the great question
that i must solve
before i die i am
buried in the college
pastry

georgie

# georgie hears from archy

dear georgie
when a first class columnist
who considers himself pretty good
who is usually bubbling
with brilliant ideas
and radiating
sweetness and light
which he feels it his
duty not to
withhold from a dejected public
starving for happiness in its dark
daily round of
misery and gloom when
i say he finds that
owing to a third helping of apple dumpling
or inability to tie his favorite necktie
or something like that
his genius has failed to produce anything
worthy of his name
then
he writes something unworthy like this
i don t usually
object to publicity in a big way
i don t mind seeing my name in print
because i
made millions in the stock exchange
or have
just successfully divorced my third wife i
am thrilled to see in red ink headlines
that i was at the bottom of the oil scandal

but i will not
permit a
driveling
pettifogging inkslinging scribbler
to sign an
unpunctuated contribution that i
never wrote
and that could never never never
be called funny
        vengefully yours


            archy

# o volstead dear volstead

boss excuse my recent
silence i have been too full
for utterance i have
been passing several
happy weeks in a cherry tree
out here on long

island bruise a cherry and
it ferments and in
twenty four hours you find
in it a kick that
would make volstead furious
from cherry to cherry
i ramble along
with my wame full of hooch
and my heart full of song
excuse me for breaking
into rhyme but it is
the influence of the cherry wine
now that the cherry season is
passing i am turning my
attention to the blackberries
i will purfle a blackberry
here on the bough
and tilt up the chalice
and cry to you how
o volstead dear volstead
the fruit still ferments
and the juices have uses
that foil your intents
you see i can t help
it boss yours for the
second coming of bacchus

                    archy

# king nicky

boss why do you not
come to your office
any more there has
been in your office
for three
days a man
calling himself nicky
romanoff who says he
is the czar of russia

and denies that
he was killed
he wants to give you
a story

for the paper
about his escape
from the bolsheviks
he has
quite a beard
and no baggage
and he is taking out
all the autographed
copies of your books
sent you by
authors and selling them
at second
hand stores
he sleeps on that pile
of newspapers
in the corner
and when he
takes off his
shoes you cannot
smell his breath
i will tell
you the truth
i do not think
he is a king at all
i think he
is the kind
of person who might if
he worked his way up
in the world
for several
years eventually
get to be
a sneak thief
or even
the lower sort of pick
pocket if you do not
come and put

him out i
will leave i am a
respectable cockroach
you must
choose between us

archy

# ode

the spring
is pulsing in
my kicks
the thing has
got me doing
tricks i sing to hell
with politics for
country hicks and
city slicks have felt
the urge
the urge of spring
the urge of spring
the urge of spring
it s trite
to say that spring
can daze
delight astonish and
amaze excite and set us all
ablaze with sidelong
gaze and passion s
rays but oh
i can
not coin a phrase
not coin a phrase
not coin a phrase
i am writing this sunday
boss but by the
time you come
into the office and
find it it

will probably be fall
and the thing will
be out of season
but i think
it s rather fine even if
it never sees the
composing room

                archy

# the tired ghost

well boss i have
finally succeeded in getting into
touch with that
ghost that loafs around here he
is a sort of tired out
timid kind of ghost and
says he wants it understood that he
is doing no haunting he hangs
around your office nights because it is
quiet he says and he hopes you
won t be harsh with him and
put him out he is hiding from a
bunch of spiritualists he
says one medium in particular
has been working him nearly to
distraction he told me some of
his experiences with
spiritualists and it is a
most pathetic tale which i
will communicate to
you later

archy

# archy mehitabel and emmet the ghost

the ghost i was telling you
about the other day is named emmet and
he is a tall thin sad looking
ghost with a long drooping
nose and a bald retreating forehead he is a
very timid ghost and
vanishes quickly at any unexpected
noise i will tell you the
truth said emmet i am a bit
    afraid of
human beings they are so
    rough i met one in the
corridor the other morning
    about three

81

o clock and he threw a heavy book right through
me later i realized that he must have
been as much afraid of
me as i was of him just then mehitabel came in
and emmet vanished it was five
minutes before i could coax him to appear
again i have always been a
bit afraid of cats said emmet cheerio said
mehitabel don t look so
melancholy gay is the word my boy tell me
the story of your life how
did you come to be a ghost anyhow emmet
was quite thoughtful for a moment and
he got sadder and sadder and then he
said i will conceal nothing
from you it was drink
that did it the story of emmet the
ghost will be continued

archy

# archygrams

industry is all right
for those who
like work for work s sake
but consider
the bee
she works like a fool all
summer and then
human beings take away
the honey she has
made
of course she wins a
great moral
victory but she cannot
eat it no one should
be trusted with
toil until he can
take it or
leave it alone at will

\*    \*    \*

i heard a man
wondering recently why
the creator made
such useless things
as cockroaches and
mosquitoes
cockroaches and mosquitoes
have often wondered

the same thing
about men

*   *   *

to a lot of
people a national
election means
a new government to
kick at and
little more

archy

# the gloomy bullfrog

boss every paper
i have seen for two
weeks has had on its
sporting page an outburst
by some impressionable
writer concerning
the beautiful legs of
m georges carpentier i
thought i would go out to
manhasset myself
and take a look at this
greek god as they have all been
calling him
though i am kind of leery of
greek gods for the
most part i used to hang around
one of these
greek restaurants a good
deal and all the god i ever
saw there
was the cash register
anyhow i says to myself
i will give the once
over to the famous leg
of m carpentier well
a half mile or so
from the training quarters of
georges i came upon a marsh and
i heard the most lugubrious
song arising from

the rushes on the muddy marsh thereof
it was a bullfrog
singing out his woe little
croaker i says to him why all this
gloom and he said
i used to have the loveliest
legs
the loveliest legs the loveliest legs
that anybody ever saw
o everybody would admire
the bullfrog s lyric limbs
the sculptor and the poet
the aesthete and the chef

they all agreed the bullfrog s legs
were just the loveliest things
but georges carpentier has come
across the roaring main

to strip the bullfrog of his fame
and now the poets sing
of nothing but the leg
of georges carpentier
le jambe
jambe
jambe
of georges carpentier
and where is all the glory
the bullfrog used to have
it is gone gone gone
outdistanced and outdone
humbled and outshone
by le jambe jambe jambe
de georges carpentier
cheer up little triller i said
alas he replied it was my only
glory and now it has been taken from me
why couldn t he have
stayed in paris
i don t wish him any ill luck
beyond what is coming to him
in the due course of his profession
but o o o
i mourn for my departed glory
and as i left there his
song was still floating over the marshes
i used to have the loveliest legs
you nearly ever saw
but now they are outdistanced
by le jambe
jambe
jambe
de georges carpentier
i left him to his grief

archy

# no literary slave

you want to know
where i have been so long well
i will tell you i
have been cutting out poetry and
making some money as
you never paid me anything for
my literary work i wandered
into a business college down the
street a few weeks ago and i
was fooling around one of the
typewriters when the
proprietor said to me if you want to
make a little money you can
do it by cleaning those
machines so he tied a piece of
cotton onto my stomach and i crawled back

and forth over the keys
till i got them cleaned i get
ten cents a typewriter for the
work and i am resting my head also i
find a certain satisfaction in being
useful of a kind that i
never felt when i was merely a poet i
may come back to literature again boss but
never on the old terms i am
taking on the typewriters in an
advertising agency to clean
next week if i could get three or four
really industrious cockroaches to
help me i think i would open a
shoe shining parlor in a
modest way i am enclosing a
dollar which i trust you will hand on
to the sun tobacco fund hoping
that you yourself will
eventually get away from writing and
go in for something honest i
am with best wishes but
your literary slave no longer

                              archy

# archy gardens

well boss i am
going out of the shoe shining and
typewriter cleaning business people
aren t spending as much
money to have their shoes shined
as before and they are
economizing and cleaning

their own typewriters or
letting them stay gummed up i
am now going in for making
window box gardens for
apartment house dwellers i put my head
down in the soil and revolve
myself till i bore a hole to
plant the seed and then i
plant it and cover it up and my
contract also calls for keep
ing the weeds chewed off even with the surface
of the soil i am working on
the shares and hope to get enough to eat
this spring and summer i can t say
i ever got that much out of my liter
ature when i used to be one of your
regular contributors yours

archy

We also find on our desk the following communication from Archy:

# the crippled cockroach

well boss i
think i will start a
cafe of my own i have a
lot of playmates who
are familiar with the res
taurant business in its most
occult phases and i
could depend upon them for
attendance if not for col
lections i shall call it the

crippled cockroach and the
motto shall be drop in boys the
onion soup is fine the
management will keep an eye

on the hats and coats but
refuses to be responsible
for the food served this
restaurant of mine will
be different yours till
they find a diet
cure for the tropic
of cancer

                    archy

# lessons of the fairies

Sir Arthur Conan Doyle believes in fairies as well as ghosts, and in his book, "The Coming of the Fairies", shows photographs of them.

With regard to ghosts, while we have never believed in them, we have always been afraid of them.

And with regard to the fairies, we put it up to Archy the Cockroach.

"Are there such things?" we asked him.

He replied:

> millions and millions
> of them i wish
> i had a dollar
> for every one
> i have killed

"Killed!" we cried, shocked. "You don't mean to say you cockroaches kill them!"

He answered:

> we cockroaches
> do not get as many
> of them
> as the spiders do
> all insects prey on them

when they can
and they prey
on insects
did you ever see a
little transparent
shrimp just out
of the water
well that is what
they look like
and they taste about
the same way
with lettuce
and sliced tomatoes
and a dash of
mayonnaise dressing
between a couple of thin
slices of bread they
should be wonderful
i wish i had a mess
of the darned things
right now

"How do you catch them?" we asked the Demon Cockroach.

He replied:

with honey
we gaum a little
honey from a wild bee
tree onto a leaf
and they come and
eat it off
and they stick fast
to the leaves
then we pounce on them
and kill them

and eat them

"This is frightful!" we cried.

Archy said:

> why get so heated
> about the confounded
> little nuisances
> that is always
> the way with
> you human beings
> you are full of
> sentimentality
> and no sense

why do you not have
sympathy with the poor
insects which these
creatures kill and eat
it is a case of
eat bug or die with all
of us i never saw
you shed any tears
over eating an oyster
or a mess of shrimps or
a half dozen frogs legs
you eat beef and mutton
and fish and pork
and all kinds of birds
without a qualm
and you would eat insects
too if you liked them

"Horrible! Horrible!" we exclaimed.

The Cockroach continued:

you think so just
because you have not
accustomed your mind
to it if you
accustom your mind
to it the fact of their
existence and the fact
that they are food
will soon become
as commonplace to you
as snails

archy

# archy bewails an absence

say look
here boss you aint going
away like that are
you without waiting to hear the
rest of mehitabel s story i don t like
to tell these things to every
body and i suppose the best thing for
me will be to go into the
silences until you come back well

don t make it too
long boss i may only be a cockroach
boss but i have the temperament of
a galli curci and
you won t hear me unless
you coax me it s lonely here without
you boss there s a
funny looking little

fellow sitting in your big chair trying
to look as if he could
cover one quarter of
it and
pegging at your
typewriter as if he knew the trick well
boss it aint the same and i wish you
were back
and so does he

               archy

# kindness

some people put the
art into
artichoke eating and
others put the choke

into it and
national gardens week will be
here pretty soon why
should not that
be a time when humans
elected to show a

little christian kindness to
us poor insects they
might plant two rows
of vegetables next
to the fence just
for us alone
yours till
the process of
fermentation is stopped
by law

archy

# believe it boss

you may not
believe it boss
but it is the solemn
truth that sometimes
you humans
are just as ridiculous
to us insects
as we insects
are to you humans

archy

the end

library of congress cataloging-in-publication data

marquis, don, 1878–1937.
archyology: the long lost tales of archy and mehitabel / by don
marquis; edited and with a preface by jeff adams, with drawings by
ed frascino.
    p.    cm.
    isbn 0-87451-745-1 (cloth: alk. paper)
    1. cockroaches—poetry. 2. cats—poetry. i. adams, jeff, 1947–.
    ii. title.
ps3525.a67a867   1996                     95–39416
813'.52—dc20